AF409133

ÉTUDE

Ukiyo-bi

Copyright © 2024 Ukiyo-bi

All rights reserved.

No part of this publication may be reproduced, distributed, or transmitted in any form or by any means, including photocopying, recording, or other electronic or mechanical methods, without the prior written permission of the publisher, except as permitted by copyright law.

The story, all names, characters, and incidents portrayed in this production are fictitious. No identification with actual persons (living or deceased), places, buildings, and products are intended or should be inferred.

Book Cover by Ukiyo-bi

Illustrations by Ukiyo-bi

First edition 2024

Contents

Lacrimosa

Full of tears will be that day
When from the ashes shall arise
The guilty man to be judged;
Therefore, spare him, O God,
Merciful Lord Jesus,
Grant him eternal rest.
Amen.

The white sky overflowed into a veil of translucent fog that covered the silent cemetery. Bare trees, the cold and he – a living creature amongst the dead; dead the same as them. Bleached hair, tired black, piercing eyes and the name Assos, written in katakana, under his left eye. He was dressed in a black uniform worn by Japanese students, with a white shirt underneath. With a book in his hand, he stood above the grave of his faithful friend – his only friend.

This vast world seemed too small that one could survive in it, so now he was dreaming peacefully in a black coffin, in the embrace of white chrysanthemums.

He used to be a poet – an excellent poet – but now just a painful reminiscence in the past of his faithful friend he remains. And all his memories, that were left behind, were now nothing more than an echo of his spirit trapped in-between two paperback covers – now in Assos' hands.

Not wanting to possess that dead child of his friend's mind, Assos spoke in agony: "Here you have it. Take it with you. Take this bastard whom nobody wanted." – His words disappeared into the grave, together with the book.

And the book leaned onto the chest from which it once wrenched free. Her fate being to disappear from this world together with her creator. All those years spent bleeding her creation were, in the end, in vain.

Assos observed her. She hypnotised him with her cries. She screamed… She wanted life. She wanted to be reborn every time somebody read her. She screamed. She cried for her creator, and her screams, her cries mingled with the sound of the raging sea.

Her owner, was just a few feet away, lying on the beach covered with darkness and with Assos' gaze. Assos was not Assos any longer, he was Lord Byron, and the corpse next to him, that of his friend Shelley. And the book, that of his friend Keats – the one he gave to Percy for his birthday.

"First John, and now you leave me too… My old friend. To die under such unfortunate circumstances, why? What shall I tell to your beloved wife? How embittered she will be to learn about your fate? – Quietly he squeezed the words through his trembling lips, with the moon revealing his teary eyes.

Deeply lost in the labyrinth of grief and remembrance of his dead friend, he collected firewood. In a delirium, he piled it up, and he put the body on the pile, and the book on the body. A spark on the tip of a match flickered in the dark for a moment, but the dark devoured it with its cold jaws, only to have that same spark be reborn in a blaze that banished the dark.

The same as the dark devoured the spark, now the flames devoured the body, together with the book.

The hot kisses of the flames were slowly burning the body. The book disappeared in the flames merging with the silver moon high up in the depths of the black sea. And out of the ashes of the book, the untamed heart of the artist emerged.

Byron awoke from the delirium into a trance. The heart called for him. Out of its unrestrained desire to create, it called. And Byron answered that call. He stretched his hand out towards the flame, feeling its hot touch, but the other voice was stronger, pooling Assos to itself.

Out of reality, Assos awoke into a dream; out of a dream he fell into waking. In front of him a teacher, and around him a forest of insidious smiles. In his ears the song of the sea still ringed, and his heart still tightened, for the loss of his friend.

Like a marionette, the teacher bounced around as she talked in anger, yet all her words disappeared in the vacuum of Assos' disorientation. And all he did was to nod confirmatively in the rhythm of the teacher's furious foot hitting the ground.

"Go, wash your face, and then return. You can't follow the lecture like that." – She commanded and he obeyed

The stench of ammonia, semi-darkness, the sound of the sea, the bonfire, the grave, the book, the friend, he as Assos, and he as Bayron. Everything was spinning. Reality and fiction were entwining in a tedious dance on the stage of Assos consciousness. The cold water run through his fingers – he observed it. It was twinkling in the dark, and its noise was returning Assos into reality. He collected the water with his hands and dived his face into it. And did it again. And again.

He lifted his head and the bright light of the neon lamp blinded him. He moved his hand over his pale face – touching the dark circles under his eyes. He left the bathroom and entered the living room clothed in moonlight. He looked at the room in detail, as if it was his first time standing there. It was a small room filled with books and paper, scattered all around the floor. Surrounded by them, a small couch, an armchair and a table, stood in the middle. On the table, just a laptop and an ashtray full of cigarette butts.

Assos lay down on the couch, took a box of cigarettes out of his pocket and lit one up. The tip of the cigarette brightened up with an orange flicker, and the blue smoke mixes up with the stale air. He observed the tip if the cigarette, observed himself out of the armchair.

"Why do you prepare my funeral?" – Assos in the armchair asked

"I do not prepare it, I already did it." – Assos on the couch answered

"All right… Why did you bury me? – Assos in the armchair asked again

"And again, you ask wrongly" – Countered Assos, with his gaze fixed at the tip of the cigarette as he lay on the couch

"Then, how should I ask you?"

"It is true that I buried you, but do not blame me. Blame those who killed you."

"It is no one's fault but yours. All the blame is on you."

"How that?" – Assos asked absent-eyed

"The same way there is no life without death, nor death without life, the same way there is no poet without poetry, no poetry without a poet. In other words, there is no Me without You…"

"And no Me without You"

Assos in the armchair nodded affirmatively with a painful smile carved into his face. Assos lay on the couch observing the cigarette as it turned into ashes. The ash breaks and falls, as thus the snow – out of the blood-illuminated sky. Assos, knee-deep in snow, stood on a meadow far from any civilisation. It was night. The smell of coal and cold pierced through his nose.

Assos breathes in wistfully and falls to his knees. He chokes in tears as the blood flows out of his wrists tainting the snow scarlet. He gives off a frightful scream. That of an agonised creature. And the scream echoes into the distance, echoes into the dark night. And he screams again, and again he is observed by the other Assos.

"Do you understand now what it means to be an artist?" – Asks his alter ego

Assos observes him mutely sobbing in tears.

"That state that you are in right now, that is the true nature of the artist. To bleed in the darkness, as one's screams are devoured by the same. For that, the artist was created, and as such he shall depart from this world." – His alter ego tells him with anger

"Exactly to avoid this pain… this suffering…" – Assos tries to respond, but his words are being lost – "That's exactly why I buried you. So, I would not have to go through all of this…"

"Because you thought that it would be better to die than to have the whole world turn a deaf ear to you."

"Yes. Yes, exactly because of that. I can't take it anymore." – Assos' shoulders shook from all the crying

"Blake…"

Assos lifts his head observing his alter ego questioningly.

"A man of the eighteenth century who bled in darkness, without anyone hearing his cries. But in the end, his cries still found ears which they could kiss."

"But I am not Blake. I am not stupid enough to waste my life in a futile act. What does he get from the fact that everyone knows his name today?"

"He doesn't, but the world does. You are not Blake, and I should not die just because of that. An artist does not create so he could benefit from his work, but so that the world could benefit from it. Which world shall it be, the present or the future, is not for the artist to decide. For him, it is to create, and only to create." – Assos tries to respond, but his alter ego forestalls him – "The world you create remains forever in the collective consciousness, and you as its creator will live forever through that world, even thou you tasted death a long time ago."

"I rather die now, than spend the rest of my life in the subconscious of the collective consciousness." - Assos opposes his alter ego

His alter ego responds: "The body burns off, but the heart continues to burn in the flames."

And again, Assos is Byron. And again, he is on that beach. And again, he hears the roaring of the sea, and again the bonfire illuminates the night. Byron observes the heart. It hypnotises him again. Byron slowly reaches for the heart, able to touch it this time. The bonfire collapses and the flames flare up into the sky. And in the sky, a red moon observes that tragic creature.

"To bleed alone in the darkness is a curse and a reward for the artist. An own hell, but an own paradise too. One which the reader can enjoy more than the writer himself. Am I not right, young Stephen?" – Asks the teacher looking at Assos with a gentle smile

"For the writer a hell, and for the reader a paradise. Of course, if the reader even exists. And if he doesn't, then neither exists the writer, nor the world. Only the bleeding, the hell, and a shell (in the form of a human being) inside that hell do then exist." – Assos replies to her

Someone puts a hand on Assos' shoulder, pressing it gently: "If there will be a reader or not, only time can tell. The artist must confront himself with the storm of ignorance, and for his bravery, he shall be rewarded."

And again, Assos is in the embrace of the fog. In front of him the grave, and in the grave he – his alter ego.

"I don't want to resist. I can't resist. Is death not a bigger bliss than the search for immortality which you might never reach?" – Assos asks now desperate, and his words mingle with the fog – become the fog

"The suffering in search of immortality is better than the life of an empty shell whose body will never rot." – An answer out of the grave

Nodus Tollens

A dream of Psyche

Whether it was a dream or reality, Ganymede never found out. It was an extraordinarily strange day, inhaling majesty and exhaling malediction. On that day, the dead sun sailed through the blue cloak and blessed the green carpet woven from life – a small grove – with its golden silk.

Hidden from their deceased master, the birds sang a hymn, praising the same, hoping for his gentle touch and warm kiss. The stream joined them, in their singing, with the murmur of water falling from stone to stone. Inspired by that divine hymn, a cricket – hidden deep within a sea of flowers, which imitated the beloved sun – accompanied them with its instrumental.

At the edge of the flowery sea, right by the stream, a large oak tree grew, stretching its branches towards the heavens, trying to grasp the life-giving sun. Someone had deceived it long ago with lies about the sun's majesty and grace. Now, in its shadow, lay Ganymede, and in his embrace, Psyche.

Completely naked, they were caressed by a warm breeze, which pleaded with the oak tree to allow the sun to gaze upon them; and the oak tree granted the request. Even though the sun barely caught a glimpse of the two, it felt shame over their beauty and, instead of dimming, it shone even brighter. And the birds cried out in their honour, and the stream began a new hymn in their honour.

On the other shore of the flowery sea, right at the beginning of the dark forest, a horrifying creature trembled. Blindfolded it stood, with buttons on the bandage where the eyes should have been. Its mouth, though sewn shut and unable to move, seemed to be grinning at the sight before it. A white shirt covering its chest, and the rolled-up sleeves revealing cuts on its forearms. On the palms of its outstretched hands eyes were drawn. It stood barefoot, wearing black, tight pants.

"Will your love last forever?" – gently asked that divine creature with blond hair that was like a wild waterfall

Hugging her tighter and resting his chin on her shoulder, Ganymede sang: "As long as this heart beats, it will be filled only with you."

"And when it stops?" - she asked, looking at him, and her eyes twinkled with innocence, more attractive than the truth - "Will you still love me then? Tell me that even then I will be your whole world." - she felt shame, and her cheeks blushed with the fragile colour of cherry blossoms

"Even when it stops, it will belong to you, and only you." - Ganymede answered her and confirmed it with a kiss onto her blue eye

Resting her hands on his chest, she gazed deeply into his azure eyes and spoke: "Swear with your life – our love – that you will love me forever.

Promise me that your love will grow forever in the garden of our unity and that it will never wither."

"And let this oak tree be my witness. And this wind that blows softly. And the birds that sing so sweetly. And let this stream be my witness. By the bright sun, I swear, my love for you will forever last."

Hearing those words, Psyche fell into his arms, burying her face into his chest, and he buried his lips into her hair.

"Then I too will love you forever. And I will be a part of you as long as there is love for me in your heart."

Divinity fallen from grace

Dressed in beauty, she lay on the cold floor. In a red dress, which she wove out of herself, she lay peacefully as if dreaming. She seemed happy. For the first time, since Ganymede knew her, she appeared genuinely happy. And all that happiness was expressed with only a gentle smile. A smile like a mirage.

"Deserved happiness, even if only at the very end, but unjustly replaced through our happiness for her sadness." – was Ganymede's first thought upon witnessing the surreal sight of that angel devoid of humanity, mixed with the sight of that petrified womb which rejected her. Losing his footing, a black veil covered the cruel reality, hiding it from

Ganymede's lost and empty gaze. Sinking deeper into the darkness, the darkness began to revolve around Ganymede, and Ganymede around himself.

Only after hearing his name repeated multiple times, which barely penetrated the darkness of the abyss, did Ganymede find himself back in the real world – face to face with a policeman whose gaze was empty and devoid of all emotion. A certain discomfort of being there – in a fragment of someone else's reality – was evident in those dull blue eyes.

"Sir... I'm asking you again, do you live here?"

"Yes... Yes... Tenant..."

"I'm really sorry about all of this, but if I could just ask you a couple of questions, so that I can take my leave. The end of my shift is near, and I still have to submit the report."

"Of course... Sorry..."

"You say you are a tenant; how long have you been living here?"

"About half a year."

"Were you close to the deceased?"

Close? Close... I slept with her. Is that close enough? - "No. Not particularly."

"I understand. However, you've been living here for – as you said – half a year – I'm guessing that your relationship wasn't just a hi for a hi."

Should I tell him? No. I am 25 years old, and she was only 16. - "I was tutoring her."

"I understand. In that case... Has she ever said anything to you that could suggest that she would do something like this? Maybe you've noticed some sudden mood swings? Or maybe you know of a note she might left; or something like that? Anything that would help us in this case."

Yes... she sent me a goodbye email. I know she had depression. I know she was self-harming. But I... - "No. Nothing."

"Are you sure? Think again. You see... In most cases, a person who decides to commit suicide leaves behind some sort of suicide note. And no one is going to kill themselves just like that, without any reason. Suicide is usually preceded by depression or some other type of mental problem. That's why I will ask you again, are you a hundred percent sure that you didn't notice anything *unusual?"*

Suicide. Such an ugly word for such a brave act. Even when a chicken breaks out of its shell, they say that it is born, so why not for a human being? - "I'm sorry. I do not know."

"It is okay. It's not your fault. However, if you remember something, don't hesitate to let me know."

"Alright."

"As far as I'm concerned, I'm done here. I will send my colleagues to..."

The policeman's voice dissipated into the empty space of silence as quickly as the darkness once again enveloped Ganymede's gaze, which, with its last strength, returned to the petrified sight by the window.

That embodiment of life and death by the window stared into nothingness – disregarding the painful reality – repeating in her thoughts: "Why? Why? Why am I so unhappy? Do I not deserve even a speck of happiness in this cruel and useless life? First, he left me... discarded me like an old rag, no longer of any use – and now you. How cruel? Did I deserve this fate? Why is it that someone must always take away from me the things for which I care about in this rotten life? Why? Why?"

Not even when they were carrying away that empty shell of her own flesh and blood did she turn around. Only Ganymede, with a lost gaze that wandered between the two men carrying, not pausing for a moment on that which they carried, escorted the young girl's body with words crafted by his unknown friend.

In darkness I stand
The darkness within me
Said the angel
And then he was born

Those who gave birth to him
And pulled him from his fleshy shell
They now bow to him
And praying to their false conscience to be free

But the noose is barbed wire

The angel in the heavens, free

Observes, with disgust, the dreadful scene
And weeps at human nature
And laughs at his own fate

His past, now just scars on his forearms

Whispers of a breeze from Eden

I had hoped that you would be my light in this darkness in which I had lost myself. I prayed to God in the hope that your embrace would save me from falling over the edge of the horrifying abyss. But apparently, I wasn't worthy of God's attention. Those hands that were supposed to save me cruelly pushed me off the cliff.

Don't worry. Don't mourn. I don't want you to feel guilty for my worthless life. I know it's not your fault, it's mine. I'm to blame for being foolish enough to think that a child could provide you with that which is reserved only for women. Surely that's why you ended up in bed with my mother.

But I would have appreciated it if you had been honest with me from the start. You could have rejected me outright instead of giving me false hope - building a house of cards just to bring it down. But I guess that's the only purpose I serve - to be a doormat to the cruel human race.

Ironically, how my name - Porphyria - so perfectly reflects my fate. The only difference between me and Porphyria from that poem is that her lover loved her, while mine was indifferent to me.

But don't worry. In all your indifference towards me, I managed to find pleasure in the sparkle of your eyes when we made love - even though that sparkle was caused by memories of another.

But don't worry. Don't mourn for me, because it's not your fault. You always kept your relationship with my mother a secret to spare my feelings, and for that, I thank you. If you want to blame anyone, blame my mother. She opened my eyes in the most gruesome way. But don't blame her either. She's not at fault. I am to blame for being born weak.

And once again... Don't worry. Don't mourn. It's not your fault. I loved you, and I will love you eternally. In this dark night, you are my shining star.

Goodbye

Funeral

On that day, the scorching carcass hung from the pale canvas. Its putrid breath cursing the life which it painfully envied. And the flame of pain that burned within the depths of its inflated being, was robbing, with scalding kisses, the life from its blinded idolaters.

In fear of his wrath, the birds remained silent, hiding deep in the treetops. Even the wind came to a halt, after witnessing the fate that, in an act of relentless fury, befall that green cover. In its blind devotion, it became like the one it adored so much.

Only the white stones that stood on the now-yellow cover dared to raise their defiant foreheads toward the omnipresent shepherd. With outstretched arms, they mocked its power over them – over those who were dead even before birth.

At the very edge of that petrified forest, a large oak tree stood with the same defiance. In its shadow, the priest, the mother, and three elderly women sought shelter, while the sinful soul of Ganymede was left at the mercy of the ruler of the heavens.

"I have never been happy without causing pain to others, nor has anyone else been happy without it being to my detriment," Ganymede thought, his gaze lost in the abyss that spread out before him – "Oh, my friend, why couldn't I save her, as you saved me? Furthermore, it was my hands that pushed her down the steep cliff into the raging sea of Hades."

"Fate is woven with a silken thread." – spoke the first old woman, jolting Ganymede out of his trance.

"If you pull too hard, it breaks." – added the second old woman.

"If not enough; it remains in place." – added the third old woman.

"The poor child didn't know..." – the first one began.

"When it was time to pull, she didn't..." – the second continued.

"And when another pulled on it, she severed it." – the third concluded.

"Should we mourn such ignorance?"

"Not ignorance, but a lack of knowledge."

"Ignorance, but not a lack of knowledge."

"Wisdom is in knowing."

"Knowing when to pull."

"Knowing when to sever."

"Fate is written into the river of time."

"But we choose it."

"Or we let the river carry us."

"Sometimes it will take us right where we need to be."

"And sometimes it will throw us onto sharp rocks."

"But often both."

"We shape our destiny."

"If you want it, then you'll get it."

"If you don't want it, then you won't get it." – they all said, laughing in unison.

For a long time, after everyone else was already gone, Ganymede still stood beside the tangible memory. In his mind, the girl's farewell words intertwined with the laughter of the three old women, awakening the memory of the words which his unknown friend had once composed.

Majestic sun,
Burning within the depths of my soul,

High up in the dark sky,
Your warmth,
A wire around my heart,
Why do you exist
When I cannot reach you?
Why do you shine
When you cannot warm me?
You exist only so I can long for you,
You shine only so I can long for your warmth.
Oh, majestic sun,
Exist, shine,
Envelop me eternally in the veil
Of sweet pain,
So that the dream of our union
May release its seductive fragrance into infinity.

Fragments of a memory

Life came from death, and was exchanged for death. A sin which Ganymede's father could never forgive him. Depriving his father of the only creature he truly loved, Ganymede allowed endless pain to spread through his father's constricted chest. And soon that pain was replaced by hatred and contempt. And the very sight of that helpless creature, so much like his mother, aroused in the father an unbearable fervour, causing him to completely turn his gaze away from the embodiment of the one he loved. And many years were to pass before the father was able to look upon the now crippled shadow of a sapling that could have become a proud oak tree. And not before the pain caused love to rot and be replaced by another.

On that day, he addressed his son with the words: "You will get a mother. Be submissive to her. Do not anger me."

And Ganymede was submissive – completely submissive. Even when she was seized with lust, at the sight of Ganymede swollen with passion, in the alienation of his room, and demanded to share that lust with him, Ganymede obeyed. And he submitted himself many more times, before, at the urging of his unknown friend, he found the strength to confide in his father. But the father broke out in anger, and drove Ganymede out of his sight. And then the pain built its nest again in the depths of the father's heart, blazing with a fiery flame. And to extinguish the flame, the father turned to alcohol.

That night, completely intoxicated with brandy and feelings, he burst into the darkness of Ganymede's room, shouting curses and accusations. And at the end, he declared: "If you like to tell such heinous lies, let those lies become your reality."

That night he lost his son – he lost his humanity.

You shell (not) be loved

She found Ganymede under the blanket, clutching his knees in painful sorrow, and in pure selfishness, she pulled him out of that womb.

"I feel lonely. I need your closeness," she spoke, and Ganymede complied, following her into the room in which Porphyria had once found them embraced – in the very same room where, so many years ago, she herself came into existence.

And soon, tainted by sin, they lay completely naked on the white bed, while anguish lay between them. And as she showered Ganymede with praises of his skill, and kissed him with declarations of her devotion, anger made love to his broken heart.

"How can I believe a single word that comes out of your mouth?" – Ganymede asked, his gaze fixed on the ceiling. At that moment, the torrent of words dried up, only her bewildered gaze remained fixed on Ganymede. Without giving her a chance to respond, Ganymede continued – "You've barely buried your daughter, and you're already in bed with me. You speak of love, yet you feel none for your own child. How can I then believe in the sincerity of your words?"

Visibly hurt by his remark, she replied: "I love my daughter above all else, and her death breaks my heart, but there's no reason why I couldn't love you too and express that love through our union."

"What you're testifying to is desire. Blind desire. And contempt, pure contempt. Towards me, and towards your own daughter. Don't you have a shred of shame? You look me in the eyes and manage to utter such lies without even blushing. A stone, not a heart, hides in your chest. No... even a stone would crack from shame. There's no need to look at me like that. I'm aware of your deeds. Porphyria confessed everything to me in an email."

"You accuse me of having no heart, but you're no better. You slept with both me and my daughter at the same time. You barely buried Porphyria, and you were already in bed with me."

"I am as guilty as you when it comes to dishonesty, but my dishonesty stems from pity. I didn't want to hurt her, even though I now realize how naive I have been. And you, out of jealousy, pushed your daughter to her death. You only wanted me for yourself, so you invited her to witness our sin. You killed her. Her blood is on your hands."

Consumed by anger, the beast spoke: "How dare you accuse me like that? I loved her more than anything in the world. She was all I had left in this world. You have no right to speak about things you know nothing about. You don't know my pain, so don't judge me." – her eyes filled with tears as she watched Ganymede, still naked, leaving their temple of sin.

"I loved her. I didn't want to kill her. I just wanted to be loved. Was that too much for me to ask? I lost him because of someone younger. I couldn't bear the thought of the same happening with you. I didn't want to kill her. I didn't. In my desire to be loved, I lost everyone who could have given me love. I am so desperate." – she cried, choking on her tears as she trembled in solitude, clinging to the bed in pain.

Lovers

Ganymede was sitting at the brutally massacred corpse of a once-proud oak tree, sipping from the water of forgetfulness, as hypocritical and painful as himself. Alone, in the company of blue smoke and murmurs, her words inflicting immeasurable pain upon him. A pain so terrible that it threatened to drown him in the depths of the truth that caused it.

What a repulsive creature I am – were his thoughts – corrupt and rotten to the core, beyond all redemption. Everything I touch dies, and everything withers under my gaze. I killed my mother, drove my father to his death, and pushed Porphyria into eternal slumber. And I wasn't much better towards her mother. It seems that only Psyche, I think, managed to resist my toxic touch. But she left me too.

I still remember very clearly, as if it had been a dream, that stormy evening when I knocked on her door, and she welcomed me into her life. And from a dark forest, she led me onto a spacious meadow, bathed in sunshine.

Our love bloomed with countless flowers, confirming its truth with sweet fragrances. A breeze fanned the flames of our love, while we quenched our thirst in the stream. Birds sang in our honour as the oak tree became our sanctuary.

I was never happier than I was then, and perhaps I have never been happy since.

And when his gaze turned to the left, in the very corner, shrouded in darkness, beauty sat, and Ganymede spoke: "Psyche...'"

Undying love

The birds celebrated the cut on the night's corpse, which foreshadowed the birth of a new day. Their song lonely disrupted the silence of the night, as the world still walked through the fields of dreams. Only two lovers – illuminated by a streetlamp – resisted the kiss of Somnia.

Lying in the bathtub, Ganymede held Psyche tightly in his embrace, and she held him tightly in hers. Leaning against her breasts, Ganymede intoxicated himself with her sweet scent. He listened to the melody of her heart, which played a hymn, while her lips sang an elegy.

"Why did you leave me? Why did you break our promise?" – Ganymede asked

Resting her face on his hair, she replied: "I never left you, and I never broke our promise. I've been waiting for you at the destination."

"At what destination? Which path?"

"Your path in search of yourself."

"But I still haven't found myself. I'm still wandering. And I'm tired of wandering."

Psyche didn't respond.

"Then you still love me?" – Ganymede asked as if emerging from a dream. – "Say that your love will last forever."

"By the fading of the night and the emergence of a new day, my love for you will be eternal. And I will be a part of you as long as there is love in your heart for me."

"Then I will love you eternally."

And as a knife gifted a kiss to their forearms, the water ignited like the sky, and the two lovers sailed into eternal sleep.

Sea of Trees

The sun appeared to be a small fireball dancing on the horizon, and the sky around it burned in a dark-red colour – turning into violet in the distance. The sea mimicked that sight, giving it an expressionistic touch through the constant movement of the waves. And as those waves moved closer to the shore, they would crush into the rocks, which stood in solitude, defying the superiority of the water.

On the shore, Misaki was sitting on a small chair with his gaze lost in the sunset. In front of him a canvas and paints, with which he tried to perpetuate the majestic sight spreading out in front of his eyes.

Surely it was a demanding motive, that asked for a lot of experience and talent to be depicted in its full beauty, but despite everything, Misaki tried his best to fulfil the last wish of his friend.

It was nine days ago, that the police informed him about Yuki's suicide. And now, lost in grief and regret, Misaki tried to atone for a sin he did not commit.

The two of them were not just friends, they were like brothers, born by the same mother in the same moment of a passing eternity – inseparable since high school.

Even back then, Misaki used to be the popular, athletic type with a lot of friends. He was always in the centre of attention, and he enjoyed it. Contrary to him, Yuki was introverted, and had no friends. Yuki was the type who would spend his breaks doing sketches in his notebook instead of socializing. He came from a wealthy family. Both his parents were never around. All they knew was work. As their divorce inevitably came, Yuki's mother expressed her wish not to take Yuki with her. So, he stayed with his father. Or rather he stayed alone, seeing his father only briefly for the holidays.

Being alone was something that Yuki was used to. However, Misaki was strangely eager to befriend Yuki. And as time passed, they became close friends.

While attending university, they stayed together in a small apartment. For Yuki, it was a time of rebellion, staying up for himself in spite of his father. He rejected the future his father had planned out for him, and instead, Yuki chose to go to a public university and become an artist.

Through all those years, Yuki suffered in silence. He did not know the reason why, but a monster had nestled itself in his heart, and was slowly feasting on his soul. The only trace that the monster left, were the scars on Yuki's forearms. Although he was always hiding them with bandages, Misaki knew the truth. He even tried to help, but Yuki wouldn't let him. In the end, it all culminated with Yuki choosing death.

He had disappeared eleven days ago. Two days later, a pair of policemen knocked on Misaki's door; one tall and thin, the other small and fat. After informing Misaki about Yuki's death, a couple of questions, and a cursory glance into Yuki's room, they gave Misaki a letter (found in Yuki's pocket) and left.

The letter was addressed to Misaki.

I apologize for my abrupt departure. I believe you would have held me back if you had known the circumstances. I'm sorry if my absence caused you concern, but I hope not too much time has elapsed between my disappearance and the moment you're reading this. My passing, I hope, will not weigh heavily on your heart. My wish is for you to heal quickly from the pain and not endure the suffering that Toro Vatanabe experienced after Kizuki's death.

I also wish that, if nothing else, my father might briefly experience the anguish of losing his son. In the event that nothing changes for him, that's acceptable too. After all, how can I expect him to grieve for a son he never truly cared about? Just like my mother rejected me, as did everyone else (except for you), my father did the same. The only difference is that he lacked the courage to admit it, neither to me nor to himself.

Do you remember the dream, I had so often?

I wake up in a room shrouded in darkness, a void with no trace of light. Devoid of windows and furnishings, the room is only graced by the presence of a single door on the far side. Though I can't perceive it in the darkness, I can sense its existence. Gradually, I approach and open it in silence.

Beyond lies a radiant day, the sky devoid of even a single cloud. The temperature is perfection itself, not too hot or too cold. Surrounding me are houses and trees adorned with dark green leaves. From the boundless, light blue sky, snow descends. Each snowflake falls gracefully, in unhurried descent. As they pirouette in the air, the sun, reflecting within them, blankets them in a radiant layer of iridescent colours.

Gazing upon these snowflakes, I experience a sense of freedom and happiness like never before, and perhaps never again.

Do you recall? I used to talk incessantly about my desire to live in a place like this. Now, after this decision, I am confident that I will find myself in such a place.

I have only two regrets.

The first is that I didn't have the chance to bid you a proper farewell. As you know I'm not skilled at saying goodbye. And that is why I'm composing this letter.

The second regret is that I never had the opportunity to capture the beauty of an Okinawan sunset on canvas. I've heard it's stunning this time of year.

*Once again, I humbly ask for your forgiveness.
Goodbye, my friend, goodbye.*

After reading the letter for the tenth time, Misaki found himself unable to move. Reclined on the sofa, he could feel all his senses dissipating – all the light, all the sounds, his whole existence. Only the sound of white noise remained, borrowing itself deep into Misaki's head.

After an unknown period of time, he was brought back into reality by the sound of the doorbell. In a state of automated motion, Misaki went to open the door, and it was only then, as he found himself confronted by that man, that he realized what had happened.

The man, without a single word spoken, entered the apartment and sat on the sofa where Misaki was previously seated. The man was in his late forties, dressed in a black suit and a white shirt, with a red tie around his neck. The man was no other than Yuki's father.

Waiting for Misaki to sit down, the man retrieved, from within his innermost pocket, a silver cigarette case adorned with an enigmatic emblem, extracting a filterless cigarette with practiced ease. As he returned the cigarette case back into the pocket, he pulled out a lighter, allowing its flame to tenderly coax the cigarette to life. It was only then that he noticed the letter. Without asking for permission, the man lifted the letter and began to read.

"He considers me a coward, and yet he is the one who couldn't take it on with life." – the man muttered obviously hurt, turning the letter back where he found it

"Do you really think that your son was a coward?" – Misaki tried to speak with an utterly calm and indifferent voice – "Do you really think that Yuki would have done this, if he had seen a way out? Are you even aware how great the pain was Yuki had to endure in his short life?"

"Bullshit." – the man in black lightly heightened his voice – "A hard life… suffering… Do you think that my childhood was easy? I had nothing. All day I would work in the fields, and in the evening, I would only get a bowl of rice – that's it. He had everything he could wish for, and yet he wasn't satisfied."

"Don't you understand that Yuki couldn't care less for your money? All he wanted was your love."

"Bullshit." – the man shook his head putting the cigarette onto the ashtray – "Love is not something you are granted; you have to deserve it. And what has he done to deserve it? He drew stupid pictures, went to a third-class school, and in the end he moved here. If he wanted my love, he should have had finished a real school and started to work in the company."

"Can I ask you something? But I expect an honest answer."

The man placed the cigarette on his lips, breathing in deeply, and blowing the smoke out through his nostrils: "Of course. Ask. I still have time; I can answer your question."

Misaki leaned forward looking deep into the man's eyes. They were filled with an empty coldness, like darkness approaching from the distance: "When you were informed about the death of your son, did you feel sad, even for a moment?"

He got quiet, getting lost in his thoughts for a second: "Society expects you to cry over the loss of your son; everything else would be odd and rejected by that same society. However, it would be a lie if I said I did. It would also be a lie if I said that I was not touched by his death. Yet I don't feel sad in the amount somebody would expect me to feel. Also, I'm certain that you, as his friend, are suffering more over his death than I'm capable of."

Disgusted by the man's words, willing to change the topic, Misaki asked: "Actually, why did you come here?"

"Isn't it obvious? Think for a little bit. My son died, and this apartment is full of his stuff. Did you really think that I would leave it to you?"

"I thought you didn't care for his stuff."

"I don't, and yet I want to take it with me. In the end, why should I justify myself to someone like you? My driver will come in half an hour – until then pack all of his stuff."

After a contemplative pause, the man withdrew a pair of ¥10,000 banknotes from his pocket and positioned them meticulously on the table. Throughout this exchange, Misaki maintained an unwavering, resolute gaze locked onto the man's eyes. Without so much as a blink, he patiently awaited the conclusion of the man's gesture. Once the man acknowledged the unflinching scrutiny, he rose from his seat and made his way to the door.

"What is the meaning of this?" – Misaki asked suddenly with his eyes still locked onto the place where Yuki's father was sitting.

"Take it as my son's half of the rent. I think it will be enough until you find another, cheaper, place to live. "

"I can afford the apartment on my own. I don't need your money." – Misaki's voice was stronger, and a certain bitterness of undermined pride could be felt in it.

"Still take the money. I don't want to own anyone anything." – After those words, the man left the apartment quickly, disappearing out of Misaki's life.

Just as Yuki's father had said, precisely half an hour later, the driver materialized at the doorstep. Dispensing with unnecessary pleasantries or idle chatter, he promptly inquired about Yuki's possessions. Misaki, offering no sign of resistance, surrendered his friend's belongings. Only the latter and one of Yuki's final paintings remained with Misaki as poignant mementos. In exchange, he discreetly tendered the twenty thousand yen, discreetly concealed at the base of one of the cartons.

As the sun was disappearing into the depths of the sea, Misaki noticed someone approaching him. Slowly turning his head, he caught sight of a girl with gentle facial features. Her long black hair accentuated her shining eyes and red lips, with a small nose in-between them. Despite the warmth, she wore a turtleneck and skinny jeans, completing the ensemble with flat shoes.

The ambient sounds were reduced to the hum of waves and the creaking of white sand beneath the girl's feet. The entire scene, with the girl seamlessly blending into her surroundings, exuded a beauty that begged to be immortalized on canvas. Unfortunately, Misaki had no canvas left, nor the skills to capture the full splendour of that sight.

Unashamed and fearless, the girl sat beside Misaki, her gaze fixed on the distant horizon. In her deep black eyes, a powerful flame burned, capable of both destroying and recreating eternity.

A scent of cigarettes and dark chocolate wafted toward Misaki. In harmony with the oceanic aroma, a completely new world unfolded – a world perfectly in sync with her beauty.

"You've got a lot of talent," she said in a melodic tone, her voice filled with warm tenderness as a soft smile illuminated her face.

"Not really. I just had a good teacher," he replied, his gaze fixed on the canvas.

After a prolonged silence, the girl sighed, "I usually come here to listen to the sea. I sit here, close my eyes, and listen to the waves hitting the coast, imagining how the same waves break into tiny drops, with the setting sun breaking its light before vanishing into the vast ocean." She pulled a box of Black Stone cigarettes from her pocket and lit one. The tip of the cigarette glowed in a light-orange hue as she inhaled the first puff. After a brief pause, she exhaled a large blue cloud into the air, then looked at Misaki and continued, "You're not from here?"

"No... Actually, I'm from Tokyo. I came here just to paint this."

"Just for one picture, you travelled all this way. Doesn't Tokyo have beautiful sunsets?"

Misaki remained silent for several moments, still focused on the canvas. "Of course, it does. I could have found a good spot near Tokyo as well, but... But this was the wish of my friend."

"He wanted you to come here to paint the sea?"

"Not me. He would have preferred to come himself, but he couldn't anymore."

"He couldn't?" The girl asked, giving him a questioning look as she shook off the ashes from her cigarette.

"Do you often listen to the sound of waves?" Misaki skilfully avoided answering the question.

"From time to time. Actually, just when I need a break from the people around me. The sound of the waves is so relaxing."

At that moment, Misaki noticed that her beauty wasn't perfect. Illuminated by the last rays of the setting sun, her face was depicted in soft colours, and in her eyes, Misaki saw the same tiredness as in Yuki's.

Now that she had lost her perfection, and Misaki knew she was real, he felt an attraction towards her. Just after losing her beauty, she became truly beautiful, and Misaki wished to get to know her better. He felt the existence of something between them, and their meeting seemed like a play of fate. A play of fate with a seed as bitter as wormwood and a flower as sweet as honey.

"How long are you staying, after you wish to rest from the people and the world?"

The girl looked towards the horizon, her thoughts drifting far beyond it. She closed her eyes, listening to the sound of waves. Misaki stared at her without blinking, waiting for her answer. She didn't speak until even the last spark of light vanished from the point of contact between heaven and sea. "Until this moment. I'm observing the sea until it gets dark. After that, all this beauty loses its magic and becomes just like the rest of the world."

"And after dark?"

"Afterwards, I usually go to a little Jazz club here in the neighbourhood. I have a few drinks and then go home." After saying that, she stood up and extended her hand to Misaki with a seductive smile. "But plans can be changed."

Even three days later, the easel with the canvas, capturing the beautiful sunset, remained stationed on the beach. On the fourth night, rain fell, unveiling the profound sadness concealed beneath

the beauty. It was a painting of the Sea of Trees –
the very painting Misaki had kept for himself.
Yuki's painting; Yuki's final destination.

Dance of the Wistful

Just like the human spirit, which first acquires a crack and then disintegrates into tiny pieces, so too did now the cloak of gloomy clouds disintegrate, revealing the fiery crimson sky. In the west, the weary sun was already slowly disappearing behind tall buildings, vying for heavenly love. That same sun, which at the same moment hints at a new beginning somewhere else, now, in this place, hints at a long, cold, and dark night full of pain and memories.

Of course, before it disappears, the sun instils hope in people with its last beautiful and warm rays. Not because it pities humans, but because it doesn't want to lose their love – the love on which it thrives. By leaving that glimmer of light, hope for a better tomorrow flickers in the hearts of people, but at the same time, a strong flame of pain and fear of the night burns within. Surviving the night and stepping into the light; hope worth fighting for, but also hope that can destroy a person.

Some of the rays are reflected in small puddles along the promenade in the city centre. In the puddles, reflections of people can be seen, and they become one with the sun's reflection. That promenade is nothing more than a paved street embraced by buildings with restaurants, boutiques, and the occasional tavern on the ground floors.

People walk along the promenade in pairs, in groups, or alone – they talk, laugh, or simply enjoy each other's company and the tenderness of the sun's touch.

A man like a shadow, lost in the depths of darkness untouched by the sun's light, moves through the crowd, but does not belong to it. Estranged from this world, yet still a part of it. Clad in an old light blue tracksuit and a worn-out brown coat under which he wears a white Polo shirt, he passes by deeply lost in thought, with a bowed head. His steps are measured, and he places his foot exactly in the centre of each paving stone.

He stops for a moment, looks around, takes a deep breath. The colourful scent of dying lives reaches his nose; a small florist at the edge of the promenade. As closing time is approaching, the florist is slowly bringing in the fragile flowers. The man in the Polo shirt approaches her, still lost in thoughts. His steps are short, and he lifts his legs with difficulty – perhaps hesitating whether to address her or not. Finally, he speaks up; he asks for white carnations (his beloved Mary's favourite flowers). Holding the bouquet of sanctity in his hand, he disappears into the crowd from whence he came like a spectre.

As night falls, under the watchful gaze of the moon, he arrives at the cemetery.

Now walking faster, he passes by the cold white graves. His gaze wanders around, seemingly uncertain, but his feet still know the way. They lead him to the lost purpose of his life – the new abode of his wife. Two small wooden pillars on the sides of a fresh mound of earth. A few blades of grass, at the very top of the mound, silently reach toward the silver moon.

"I said I would come, didn't I?" he utters in a soft voice, placing the bouquet of carnations on the grave. Right where another bouquet had already withered.

Sitting on the damp ground – beside the modest grave – he listens into the night. The moon sails through the dark sky, illuminating the world abandoned by the sun. Out of the distance echoes the prickly barking of a dog, mingling with the rough sound of the wind weaving through the leaves of trees. A warm flash briefly appeared and disappeared in the darkness, continuing its life as an orange flicker atop a cigarette emerging from behind a cloud of blue smoke.

He exhales the smoke through his nose, directing his gaze towards the dim moon, and speaks: "I traverse this world – through darkness. With your death, the light that illuminated this world of mine, full of pain and suffering, vanished. Was it truly necessary? Did you really have to leave me alone? Once again... Do you think I am capable of surviving without you? I terribly fear that I am not. I dread death, and you were the only barrier between our sad union. If only you could tell me what its kiss is like. Is it bitter, or is it sweet? You know... When I learned that our parting was near, I promised myself that your death would not catch me by surprise. I thought I had enough time, that I could come to terms with that fact. If nothing else, I could mentally prepare myself for that moment. How could I have been so foolish? No matter how hard I tried, your death ripped the ground from beneath my feet. I fell into the darkness of the abyss. I spent countless nights wandering in taverns. I drank and cried; cried and drank. I tried to drown the memories of you with alcohol, but it was futile. I..." – he couldn't continue the sentence. The words simply disappeared, so he just smiled at the great moon.

At that moment, as melancholy overtook him, rain began to shower the earth. Tiny, warm drops descending from the clear sky reflected the cold outline of the moon. They streamed down the face of that wretched creature, mingling with bitter tears. Everything fell silent, only the faint tapping of rain and quiet sobs echoed through the cemetery.

He took out his phone from his pocket, searched briefly, and eventually found the desired piece of music. That piece was Miles Davis' "Blue in Green" – his beloved Mary's favourite.

"Do you still remember this song?" he murmured through his lips.

After playing half of the composition, he stood up and started to dance. Dancing in circles, engulfed by rain and tears, receiving the sympathy of the night shepherd and his flock.

"Soon, my love! Soon..." – he cried out to the heavens.

Confession

Like the sword of Damocles, my unspoken words still hang over my head. If they remain unspoken, my fate is cursed; if I speak them, my fate is cursed.

I cannot recall the last time I crossed that threshold, words I long to speak, yet I hold back. I am branded by that memory, by words spoken that day – words that I accepted through silence as my only response.

Two years have passed – perhaps a little less. The world had already been reborn, heralding the joyful news with the scent of blossoms. And now the world still sleeps in the stillness of dusk, mirroring the stillness of my soul. Flakes break off from the grey mantle and fall like ash, disappearing before they touch the ground. Trees reach with their bony fingers toward the mantle. Perhaps they want to tear it apart and bask in the sun, to bloom with blossoms.

And now I stand at that same threshold and observe that familiar scene. He sits on the couch next to the fireplace – his swollen body devoid of the sweet nectar that abundant life offers. His brown eyes are sunken, dull, devoid of lustre, like the eyes of the dead. Surrounded by dark circles, they accentuate the yellow of his eyeballs. His thick, cracked lips tremble as he draws on a cigarette, and his yellowed fingers gently caress the wrinkles around those same lips.

He is unshaven. Truly an unusual sight. I remember a time when every morning he would sing as he went to the bathroom, meticulously removing even the slightest trace of beard. Now his beard is longer than his hair. Although, to be honest, cutting it shorter would mean shaving his head.

She, in the kitchen, welcomes me with a gentle smile. Her tiny eyes tired but full of life. Perhaps they simply flicker with joy now that she finally sees her son again. Even the small wrinkles around her eyes and lips seem to rejoice.

She is thin and looks much older, but she still carries herself elegantly and radiates a pride that is not in the least pretentious. And her demeanour is even more striking in comparison to that man who lacks any semblance of dignity in his posture. They truly are an odd couple.

"So, you remembered you have a home?" he says with a faint smile.

"I'm glad to see you too. How are you, mother?"

"How long has it been? Two years?"

"Something like that. I would have come earlier if I had could."

Of course, that's not true. I didn't want to come, but compelled by my mother's pleading and my own need to speak out certain words, I had no other choice.

"I know, I know. You can't get away from work. Damn private companies. It wasn't like this in Tito's time."

I remained silent.

"Have you found a girlfriend?"

"Not yet."

"Why not?"

"I don't have time."

"You have to."

"But I don't have time."

"Nonsense. I was already married at your age."

"Forget it. He'll find one," a voice came from the kitchen.

"I want grandchildren too. To play with them while I'm still alive."

Perhaps this is the right moment to utter those fateful words, which tighten around my neck like a noose, making it hard to breathe. I have nothing to lose. I'm a loser anyway. At least I would sleep peacefully tonight.

But maybe I should stay silent. Let tomorrow dawn in ignorance. Don't spoil their joy on the eve of the holiday. After all, ignorance is bliss. And tomorrow, after the rituals are over – before I leave – I will utter those words that torment me.

When I was a child, my mother would wake me on this day with a soft whisper, caressing my face, and I would just nod and lie there until she came again. And she would stroke me again, whispering a reminder that it was time.

Now, with that childhood, and the innocence that accompanies it, lost, the obligation of timely awakening was solely mine.

And the obligation of impatient waiting – in my childhood as it is now – was solely his.

Stretched out like a peacock, he stands quietly in the courtyard, observing the world that is just beginning to awaken. A gentle smile flickers on his face as his lips firmly hold the cigarette. He separates the two only to flick off the ash.

Some things never change. As a child, I witnessed this same scene. The same leather jacket, the same grey cotton pants, the same movements, the same humming, the same gaze.

But while in the past I responded to this scene with a smile, now I refrain. His words from two years ago echo in my mind. Unsolicited, he cursed my arrival, claiming that no day was worse than the day of my arrival, and believing that this didn't hurt me enough, he expressed a wish for my unbornness.

Now he is cheerful, completely unaware of his words. Tossing the cigarette butt on the floor, he wishes me good morning and moves on. I follow him, always two steps behind.

While in the past this was out of shame, out of discomfort caused by contact with people, today it's out of my reluctance to engage in conversation. If there were to be a conversation, I wouldn't be able to keep silent about what torments me so. And speaking about it now would ruin this day for all of us. And so I will keep silent and wait. When lunch is over, when the time of my departure approaches, then I will speak. And in that way, I will avoid the discomfort of shared vigil caused by feelings of injury.

Still feeling hurt, I walk behind him in a defiant effort to comply with his wish expressed two years ago.

I follow him to the mosque – it's half empty. In the past, we used to perform the prayer back-to-back, but now we have more space beside each other than is good.

I pray beside him. I listen to the sermon about the importance of family, about the imperative placed on obedience to parents. About love and forgiveness.

Maybe I'm wrong in my anger. His words, as hurtful as they were to me, seem insignificant to him. Surely he didn't say them intending to hurt me. Perhaps it was just a whim, just thoughtlessness in a moment of anger. And as unjustified as that anger was, maybe I should still forgive.

But did those words, echoing through the mosque and my heart, mean anything to his ears? Does he understand the importance of family in the same way? Do admonitions about severing family ties mean the same to him? Does he have enough love in his heart to unconditionally give it to me? I fear not.

And how can I expect unconditional love from him if I haven't given it to him? But maybe it's not too late. I still have time to show him, although, after today's conversation, I won't expect the same in return.

But in this way, maybe I'll still be able to avoid the situation he is in now. Standing over his father's grave (where we went after the prayer), his face distorted with pain.

"I miss him," my father speaks softly. "After so many years, it still hurts. Maybe he wasn't the best father. He would sit by the stove and drink all day. But I didn't have another father. I just hope I'm a better father than he was."

I don't know what to say, so I remain silent.

Like the sword of Damocles, my unspoken words still hang over my head. If they remain unspoken, only my fate is cursed; if I speak them, I will curse my parents too. So, I say nothing. I conceal my essence; let its hiding slowly consume me.

Ignorance is bliss, and I am a complete stranger to them, so let them be blessed.

Now I return to my world. A world they don't know. A world they may never know.

The nature around me still sleeps in its stillness. It faithfully reflects the stillness of my soul. Flakes break off from the grey mantle and fall like ash, disappearing before they touch the ground. Trees reach with their bony fingers toward the mantle. Perhaps they want to tear it apart, to bask in the sun, to bloom with blossoms.

Or maybe they want to embrace it.

Story

The skies and the clouds dance passionately inside the vortex of union embraced by the music of the endless night and the song of the small creatures that worship the summer moon.

Two rivers flow. They unite. Intertwine. They change their current and divide. And they merge anew. The river flows scarily into the wild ocean. The ocean squeezes the river. It lets the river go, only to greet it back into union.

Branches, with their soft touch, move across the trembling sky. With pauses, they whisper a torrent of oaths and sighs to the sky. The moon responds with a faint shine.

In the ocean, a geyser sends a greeting to meet the sky.

The world holds still for a moment, the geyser touches the sky, and the sky responds with rain. The wind and clouds unite and last as day and night – until the night leaves the stage to the day, in anticipation of the coming night.

The cruel sun wakes, from its slumber, the pitiful creature – the HUMAN – and confronts him with the BLACK STAR, which trembles in the corner of the room, observing him with its buttons. A skinny face, stitched mouth, bandages around the head with buttons in the place of eyes. On it a white shirt with rolled-up sleeves and tight black pants. It was barefoot. Its arms stretched out, with cuts on the forearms. On the stretched-out palms, a pair of eyes was drawn.

On the other half of the bed, the body was missing, but its place was filled with memories. The body will return, but will not find the expected.

Friday.

A yard. A house and a tower. The CREATURE'S beautiful voice pronounces the words of GOD. The yard overfull with CREATURES. They, filled with false piety, line themselves up and perform the rehearsed movements, pronouncing the words which they learned by heart (without knowing their meaning).

Amongst them the HUMAN. Contrite, with the head bowed, he suffocates under the pressure of the divine. The HUMAN is a sinner – the CREATURES are sinners as well. The sin of the first one is terrifying; the others will not forgive it.

DOES **GOD** FORGIVE THE UNFORGIVABLE?

The HUMAN sits amongst the CREATURES listening to the reminders. One photon after another separates from the HUMAN, in groups they ascend, transforming into blue transparent butterflies who, with trembling flutters, go to meet the sun. They gather in groups, transforming into blue birds and fly into the blue sky. In search of God, they dive into the depths of the sky.

God is distant and unreachable for sinners.

To sinners, **God** is closest.

The blue birds unite in the blue sky transforming back into the HUMAN in the yard.

A crowd of CREATURES, tall and grey, in black suits and faceless, push each other so they can flee into sin, before reuniting again out of habit. On Friday. The HUMAN is in the crowd, as well as the BLACK STAR. Trembling it observes him with its buttons.

Passing through the stone forest, which the CREATURES built for themselves as a cage to stay **civilised**, the HUMAN looks at his reflection in the shop windows. He himself is but a tall grey creature in a black suit and no face. The truth is a narrow noose around his neck, and the wind laughs cynically at his realization.

By the side of the road, an old woman sits. Dirty and wrapped in rags she cries with an outstretched hand. A coin falls out of the HUMAN'S hand, into the hand of the old woman. A **good deed**.

One good deed cannot erase a terrifying sin, nor bring about GOD'S forgiveness, but it can bring GOD'S mercy.

The old woman's warm smile is forgiveness. Only those enveloped in ignorance do forgive.

The old woman stands up and the BLACK STAR she becomes. Trembling it observes the HUMAN as he leaves.

GOD
        Love
            Human
                Love Hate
                    Human

            Life
       Death
    Life

Freedom. Captivity. Peace. Fear. Sin. Forgiveness. GOD. Human. Beast. Life. Death. Paradise. Hell. Eternity. Punishment. Reward. Pain. Emptiness. Numbness. Insignificance. Blade. Skin. Blood. Pain. Happiness. Sadness. Emptiness. Sin. Punishment. Wound. Scar. Imprecation. Despair. Thought. Fear. Loss. Emptiness. Death.

"In the Name of God—the Most Compassionate, Most Merciful.

All praise is due to God—Lord of all worlds,

The Most Compassionate, Most Merciful,

Sovereign of the Day of Recompense.

It is only You that we worship and only of You we ask for help.

Guide us to the straight path

The path of those upon whom You have bestowed favour,

not of those who have evoked Your anger or of those who are astray."

"God does not require of any soul more than what it can afford. All good will be for its own benefit, and all evil will be to its own loss. Our Lord! Do not punish us if we forget or make a mistake. Our Lord! Do not place a burden on us like the one you placed on those before us. Our Lord! Do not burden us with what we cannot bear. Pardon us, forgive us, and have mercy on us. You are our only Guardian. So grant us victory over the disbelieving people."

The HUMAN sighs "**Allahu Akbar**" and falls in prostration. He struggles with tears, and in the corner of the room, the BLACK STAR stands.

The sun bids farewell to the people, and the moon greets them. The world boils and gets lost in millions of thoughts - in one thought.

The white room is painted in orange mixed with a bit of red and a hint of purple. The HUMAN sits on a brown couch. His eyes are red from crying, but the tears have long since dried up. He curses himself. Screams. With each scream, he grips the knife tighter in his right hand. He watches the BLACK STAR and smiles painfully at it. It trebles and looks at him with its buttons.

The HUMAN rests the knife on his left forearm, and the BLACK STAR trembles even more as it moves its sewn lips, trying to open its mouth. One thread after another bursts and blood begins to flow down its chin. Tearing off the last thread, the BLACK STAR starts to scream. Its voice penetrates louder and more painfully while shaking convulsively.

"Oh God, forgive this worthless slave of Yours for his weakness. La ilaha illallah. "- uttering these words, the HUMAN pulls the knife over his skin, and the blood begins to gush in all directions.

The BLACK STAR screams savagely, raising its trembling hands toward the bandage, and rams its black-painted nails underneath it. At that moment it stops, and in complete silence, it plucks

the bandage from its eyes, and the HUMAN looks
himself in the eye.

Life of a Man

Once upon a time, there was a man…

And with his last breath, the curtains drew onto
this insignificant story he called life.

The Strange Case of the Jones Family

It was in the month of April that I arrived from a long journey just to find our family farm shrouded in silence. You could not hear the cattle cry, nor the birds sing. And there was no wind, though I do not remember a day without, at least, a mild breeze. There was no one on the fields, and I could find no one in the stable. However, the fields were not abandoned and the cattle were taken care of.

I walked inside the house calling out – proclaiming my arrival in hope of bestowing happiness on the faces of my family, but futile. No one seemed to be at home, or no one seemed to care. The first one was unlikely, for someone always stays at home to take care of the animals, and the second one was ridiculous, or so I thought--hopped.

I found my mother kneeling in the kitchen, next to the refrigerator with the door of the freezer open. A blissful smile engraved on her face as she looked at something in her hands wrapped in foil.

"Welcome back my son." she chirped in her silky voice with her eyes anchored to her hands, not daring to lose the foil out of sight.

"Where is everyone?" I asked.

"Here… They are here. I'm certain they are somewhere in the house." she answered not appreciating me of a single look.

"Shouldn't someone be by the animals?"

"Are they not fed?"

"They are, but they are awkwardly silent."

"Don't worry. Anna will take care of them."

"I know you employed her to help out, but should not someone help her out? And tell me mother, what is it in your hands that is so important that you cannot spare a single moment to look at your son?" I walked closer as I asked, curious to see what she was holding.

"The most delicious pizza in the world." she answered with a cold voice.

And as I looked at that piece of frozen pizza, an eerie shiver ran down my spine. I don't know if I was disgusted by that frozen piece of pizza or repelled by my mother's behaviour, but I walked out of the kitchen leaving her alone to observe that precious treasure of hers.

I wanted to go upstairs to my sister's room, but, halfway up the stairs, I was stopped by a familiar voice: "My son, you have returned."

Overcome by happiness I turned around to greet my father just to find myself eye to eye with something that resembled him in shape, and yet did not feel as such. He had a bucket, like a helmet, hiding the upper part of the head. I could see bandages underneath it. His eyes were red with blood, and his lips swollen and purple. It was a grotesque scene, as if from a third-rate horror movie. And yet, it was real.

Struck with confusion I asked: "Are you all right, father?"

"Yes, I am." he answered, with saliva dripping down his chin.

"Are you sure? Why the bucket on your head? You look silly."

"Everything is fine. Nice to have you back." he said and walked away.

I stood there for a few moments, trying to comprehend what just happened. It all seemed surreal to be true. I even thought that it might be just a dream.

Seeing all those strange things unfold I was frightened to see what might await me in my sister's room. My hand was heavy as I hesitantly knocked on the door. And I was startled when I received the permission to enter. It was not because I was afraid that my sister wouldn't let me in, but because I thought that she might have changed as well.

I opened the door and the light flooded the room which was shrouded in darkness. But the light was fleeting. My sister commanded me to close the door, and so the darkness took over. Complete darkness, except for the flickering blue light emitted from the computer monitor.

"So you have finally returned." said my sister.

"Yes."

"Have you seen our parents?"

"I have, but I don't understand. What has happened?"

"I don't know. One day they had a fight. It seems father was unfaithful to our mother."

"Unfaithful? You mean he cheated on her?"

"With Anna."

"I can't believe. But what happened?"

"I'm not sure. All I know is that father didn't come home for three days after the fight. And when he returned…"

"He was like that?" I pointed with my thumb to the door implying our father.

She nodded and said: "He never sleeps. But I guess that is nothing strange now. Since his return, I haven't slept either. But it is strange that he walks around the house – all the time. He doesn't eat, he doesn't rest. All he does is walk around like a wraith."

"And the bucked on his head?" I asked.

"I don't know. But have you seen how swollen his face is? I guess it has something to do with that."

"And what's wrong with mother?"

"Is she staring at that piece of pizza again?"

"She didn't look at me, not even once."

"Two days after they had that fight, she made pizza. But she was the only one allowed to eat it. And I was watching her as she did. She was crying heavily, and yet she had a grin engraved from ear to ear. She said that the pizza was so good that she had to preserve a piece to remember it forever. And since then, she is staring at it--putting it away just to let it freeze again."

"But why haven't you done anything to stop all of that?"

"What could I possibly do, when they don't even notice me?"

"I don't know. All of this feels unreal to me. Like a bad joke."

"I feel the same way. It is as if I'm trapped in the Twilight Zone. But all of this is real, utterly real."

"And Anna? What is with her?"

"Nothing. She seems completely normal. Must be something affecting only family members."

"So, you think I could become like them too?"

"Not exactly like them, but I'm sure you will undergo some changes as well. Take me for example. I haven't slept for weeks, and yet I don't feel sleepy. Neither have I eaten in that period, nor do I feel hungry."

And indeed, it happened exactly as my sister said it would.

Over the period of the next few days, I slowly lost my appetite. All the time I felt like having a stone in my guts. Even when I wanted to force myself to eat, I couldn't gulp down a single bite. This turn of events didn't bother me too much, for I had no signs of malnutrition.

On the other hand, I started having nightmares. Though I would forget them the moment I woke up, the feeling of fear, they would give birth to, would creep inside of me for the rest of the day. And every time I would remember that breath-taking fear, a shiver would run up my spine bringing tears to my eyes.

I tried to avoid sleeping, but it was futile. No matter how much I tried, eventually, it would happen and the nightmares would return with their gift of immense fear.

Over the period of the next ten days, I slowly started to feel hunger again. Yet, no matter how strong the hunger got, I found myself unable to eat. That is, if we exclude paper and frogs (still alive). I don't know the reason why, for the paper tasted dull as his innocent colour would suggest and the frogs obnoxious as it was to expect, but I couldn't help myself other than to eat.

Except for that, everything was the same as the moment I returned. My mother would be kneeling in front of the refrigerator with that peace of frozen pizza in her hands, wearing her blissful smile. My father would relentlessly walk around the house not responding to the world around him. My sister would stay in the safety of the darkness begotten by her room tirelessly staring at the screen of her computer.

All their acts were performed with such dedication and awe that it seemed as if they were worshiping some kind of an all-powerful god. But that god was not one of love and mercy, but rather one of fear and utter despair. Perhaps not a god, but a vicious demon instead.

The only person that still seemed to behave normally was Anna. And that, only for the fact that she was still doing all her duties. On the other hand, in all this period, since my return, I haven't seen her once. Until one day, that is.

I was getting ready to catch some frogs when I heard a cry and a shallow noise. I ran out to see what had happened. In front of the stable Anna was lying in a puddle of blood. My father crouched above her, poking, with an axe, pieces of her skull out of the spilled-out brain.

I looked at the brain, and a desire to eat it awoke inside of me. I was convinced that it would taste heavenly, but the pieces of bone inside of it repelled me. So I turned around and ran inside the house to call for help. I couldn't find my mother, and my sister was unwilling to come out of her haven of darkness. So I returned, at least, to take my father away from the poor woman's body.

However, on my return, he was already dead. His body lying next to Anna's. The helmet was off, revealing what was hidden beneath. Cancerous pinkish growths all over the right side of his face. And I realized, it truly was not my father who was lying there, but a grotesque creature twisted to resemble him.

At that moment something broke inside of me. The sadness, which was creeping up within me, was suddenly gone. All those questions, and all that confusion that I felt just moments ago, gone. And my wish to bury the two bodies, was also gone. So I just returned inside, as if nothing had happened.

I found my mother kneeling in the kitchen, next to the refrigerator with the door of the freezer open. She was crying heavily as she looked at that piece of frozen pizza. And, like a chant, she was repeating: "Was this not the best pizza in the world?"

Deep inside I knew, I should feel pity for that poor creature. I wanted to utter some words of consolation, to comfort her, but I found myself unable to speak. Unable to approach her as well.

Over the next few days, silence descended upon the farm. My sister was still unable to find her way out of the belly of her room. My mother was still kneeling in front of the refrigerator, crying over that piece of pizza. And the two bodies, lying outside, unchanged by the will of nature.

For me, all of that became unbearable. I wanted to scream, to cry, to finally wake up from that nightmare. But I knew that it would not happen as long as I stayed. So I decided to go, and never return to that cursed place.

And indeed, once I was gone, everything started to go back to normal. My craving for frogs and paper was no more. And my nightmares were no more. And all those emotions that died at the farm, were now born again.

And it was not until many years later, as I learned of the death of my mother, that the nightmares returned. However, this time my memories of them would not dissolve into oblivion, but would stay to haunt me even during the day.

"You whore! You bloody whore!" my father screamed at my mother who was kneeling in front of him.

"Don't… Don't speak those harsh words." my mother said crying.

"How could you do this to me?"

"I… I didn't."

"Oh, you didn't? So I'm a bloody liar?"

"No… Please, you have to believe me."

"What to believe you? That it was just a mistake? That you didn't know what you were doing? That you still love me? What?"

"Yes, just a stupid mistake. You know I love you; that I would never hurt you on purpose. Please, forgive me."

"You bloody whore!" he slapped her with such an intensity that she fell to the ground. "How dare you look me in the eyes and ask for forgiveness? I gonna kill that lesbian whore of yours. And once I killed her, I gonna kill you. So better run while you still can."

As my father turned around to go find Anna, my mother took a big stone and hit him on the head. And as he fell to the ground, she hit him again. And again. And again.

She did not stop until the scull broke and the brain spilled out on the ground. And as she realized what she had done, she screamed. And in her despair, she tried to gather the pieces of his brain together, repeating in a trance: "I'm sorry. I'm sorry. I love you."

Then I saw Anna taking the bloody hands of my mother whispering in a gentle voice: "Everything will be alright. Don't cry. I can repair him."

"But he is dead." my mother said.

"He is just broken. Don't worry, I can fix it."

"How?"

"Don't worry. I will fix it."

"But how?"

"You just take this brain and eat of it. Maybe make a pizza. You like pizza. And once you are finished eating, he will be repaired."

"Promise?"

"I promise. By the sin of our love, I will repair him." Anna said and kissed my mother tenderly.

Three days later it was done. My mother had eaten the brain, and my father had returned as a reborn man. And it was at that time that the whole madness started. The strange case of my, the Jones, family.

The Sun is a Being in All of Us

The song "Awake" pulled me from my slumber.

The clock read 1:30, and the radio emitted white noise. That song was just an echo in my mind. Just the remainder... Yes, a remainder.

The room was supposed to be shrouded in darkness. Complete darkness that extinguishes every life. Darkness which is the beginning and the destiny of us all. It follows us throughout our lives. It's always with us, and in the end, it remains the only one with us. But now it wasn't so. Light was evidently seeping in from outside.

I could have opened the window and looked. Found out what was going on, but I didn't. I rose from my old bed and headed outside. My head was heavy, and I felt pressure on my chest. Maybe it would have been better to lie down again. But no, curiosity was stronger.

Through the small hallway – where the familiar darkness prevailed – to the front door.

Outside, everything was bathed in warm sunlight. The cold, white rock cliffs, rising not far from my house, had acquired a slight, almost imperceptible yellow hue. The vivid green leaves of the trees that surrounded us now had an idyllic dark green colour; the sky was also a dark blue. Even the air itself took on a warm hue, recognizable only as a beautiful, gentle feeling. It smelled intoxicatingly fresh. So beautiful that you could get lost in it.

What's happening? How is this possible? Is this just a dream? High in the sky, tilted toward the north, stood a huge sun.

"No, this isn't a dream. Apollo is playing with our senses." - a voice said and disappeared, still echoing in my mind.

And indeed. This wasn't the real sun. It just looked like the sun. But different. Bigger and more beautiful. It had no flaws or imperfections. It stood in the sky as if it wanted to show us a better world. A world without our intimate darkness. With not even a shadow existing. Everything was illuminated. Harmony and balance prevailing.

Yet the whole city was in deep slumber. I was the only one who saw this divine gift. I was the only one who felt the beauty of the new age. There was no one with whom I could share this moment, no one to feel what I felt, to see what I saw, to be part of both the end and the beginning at the same time.

"Surrender to the light. Let the light permeate your entire being. Become light." - a voice said and disappeared, still echoing in my mind.

To become part of the light. To close my eyes and let the light pass through my entire body. All the way to the deep-hidden darkness. If darkness no longer exists anywhere, then let it not exist within me either.

When I closed my eyes, again there was only light. I felt the light embrace every part of my body.

These were the same touches as the touches of darkness. Only darkness was cold, and light was warm.

I felt the light take me in. I felt everything around me disappear. The cliffs, the trees, the houses. None of it existed anymore.

Now there is only light. Light is eternal, omnipotent, and omnipresent. Light becomes a part of me, and I become a part of the light.

"Be the light." - a voice says and disappears, still echoing in my mind.

To be the light? I have become light. All-encompassing and warm, yet people still live in cold darkness.

Pathogenic

As the night falls over this wretched world and as the sun leaves us to our misery, sirens cry out admonishing us with their shriek.

What horror-inducing sound this is. I dread every eve and every morning anticipating the siren's wake, only to shudder anew when those alien sounds the silence break. Not even in my dreams I can find a haven from their grasp. Oh, how tired I am of this fear.

Yet those sirens are not the only sound of which my heart shivers in dread, for once they stop a solemn voice, inducing calm through authority, protrudes through the air. The curfew is now in place." – it proclaims – "It will stay active until sunrise. All trespasses will be punishable by death." And every time I hear those words, a part of my soul breaks away into the abyssal depths of our oh so sublime humanity.

And despite the commandment being uttered, many pious people will gather tonight in front of the Church to worship the gods and bring a sacrifice to that deity of chaos and destruction. A deity whose name, in a language long forgotten, brings nothing but madness and utter despair.

All of that in hopes of finding solace in these times of disease; of finding tranquillity which only the divine can bring about in this profane world.

And although my heart, being torn apart by angst yearns for comfort, I shall not go. I must not go! I must clinch to my humanity – the broken pieces that still remain of it.

I will be a sentinel in this dark night of the ego. A whiteness to the night of the id that holds us tight in its grasp. Praying for our humanity to be restored, as our sins are cleansed in fire.

But is the cleansing not a sin in itself?

*

Contrary to the declaration he made in his soliloquy, he fell asleep. And he slept until the sirens shook him out of his unsettling dreams. And it was not until the sun had sprung from the eastern sky – high above the decrepit remains of the city – that K. embarked on a walk to perpetrate his daily tasks. Although he might have phrased that in a more self-deluding way.

He lived on the second floor of a half-demolished three-story building. However, the stairs, passing his apartment, were leading into nothingness. Even the wall, which should have been on the other side of the stairs, protecting the opposite apartment from curious eyes, was missing. And half of the floor of that apartment had crumbled away. And even the apartment above was entirely missing, leaving no cover, no hindrance for the gaze to reach the sky.

It was not the best of living spaces, lacking in safety and deprived of cosiness, but K. knew he still had more than others did – a roof and four walls to call home. For many, the apartment on the opposite was reality. And as if that was not enough of reality, the area, with most of such housing being the norm, was a dangerous one. A no-man's land filled with those who have lost their last traces of humanity, transcending into the realm of demons.

On the opposite side, there were those living in complete opulence with no luxuria left unsatiated. The world, which such individuals inhabited, could be compared to Heaven or be simply called Universe 25.

And as for K., as he descended the stairs and entered onto the street, he was met with *Homos*. Those people, like ants, navigating in between the walls of half-damaged buildings, each with their goal in front of their eyes. Engaging in conversation or trade; offering or taking services or simply acknowledging each other's existence with a simple look. And all of that in the attempt to imitate normality, a way of life long lost in a time before the miasma.

Now one of them, K. moved down the street. The very street in which he had spent and, eventually, lost his childhood. The light-brown facades with their yellowish tinge, the cobbles covered in yellowish dust, and even the people's faces yellowish of dirt seemed to protrude from the past untouched by time. Even the laughter and joy seemed to be the same as those from long ago. Only he had changed. Once an ignorant child filled with joy, now he seemed an adult weary with angst.

It was a beautiful day, with the pale blue sky stretching endlessly, the sun shining gently and a mild breeze dancing around the streets. The birds were singing their hymn. And even the so dreaded church appeared pleasant.

It was a large building in the Gothic style, placed on a wide, open area, on the right, at the end of the street. Its colour was that of the city, as was that of the few islands of grass which were surrounded by a sea of sand. On the left, near the metal fence, a dead tree stood firmly, reaching into the sky. On the right, the remains of a pyre, used in the sacrificial act of last night.

It was five years ago, at the time when K. was only sixteen, that he witnessed his first sacrifice. An event so traumatic, rendering the attempt to participate in another one a sheer impossibility.

He still remembered that night vividly. The crowd, the darkened silhouettes jostling to get a better view. The Subdued chants ringing in his ears. The priest, in his orange, red and gold robes with a pointed headpiece falling over the back and sides of his head, while the front was covered by a gas mask. A tube protruding from the mouth and leading to his back. The large black eye pieces observed each soul carcfully as he mumbled the words of his sermon. Behind him were two deacons, clothed in the same manner, but their robes being red, and orange, having less ornament. Each of them was holding a rod. And on top of each rod, three candles were placed. On their bodies, covered in the warm light of the pyre, shadows were dancing lively.

On the pyre, a naked woman was being eaten by the fire. Her firm breasts, her slender waist, and her ethereal muff were presented sensually to the gluttonous eyes. And those same, who once searched solace in her bosom, were now calling her trumpet. Yet, the only word by which K. could call her was sister.

Ever since the death of their parents, she has been both, mother and father, to that little boy. She raised him up selling her body, even sacrificing it in the end – unwillingly – to the gods. And even with her last breath, she prayed for her brother's wellbeing.

K. carefully navigated through the streets – through and out of the sea of bodies. Navigated his way into a less frequented area, a purgatory in between the realm of those whose eyes are yet to be opened and the realm of those who upon losing their humanity, had their souls contorted in the flames of the infernal abyss known as reality.

Here, all the buildings were ground level, with only a few, through the remains of a wall fragment, alluding to former height. Most had no door, but a curtain hiding the inner world from that which lurked on the outside. And they were with windows broken or completely missing (replaced by nylon foil).

As K. moved through the streets, covered in dirt and dust, under the scorching sun, he encountered only a few of the decrepit souls inhabiting those also decrepit homes. Sitting crouched, in front of them, they stared into nothingness, with dull eyes and empty gazes, showing no interest in K., nor the bag he carried in his hand. And with the same eyes, he was met even by those two copulating in an alley as he passed behind them. They all seemed already dead, just waiting for death.

His way led him further into a rundown house, and into a studio apartment behind a wooden door. Inside, the air was stale. The sharp stench of urine entwined with the sweetness of rotting flesh were a weight on K.'s chest, making every breath an endeavour. The room was scarcely filled. And old white wood-burning stove to his left and a sink next to it, with a window above. To his right, a divider, also in white, but blathering; separating the toilet area from the rest of the apartment. In front of him a small table, brown in colour, and behind it an old half-ruined couch with a scrunched female figure lying on it under a blanket.

"Sorry for letting myself in just like that." – K. spoke looking for a place to sit – "How are you feeling today?"

She saw his wandering eyes and pointed with a half nod to the table: "Please sit. Felt cold… Had to burn the chair. Wasn't sure you would come back."

K seated himself on the table taking another look around the room. There was no carpet, just old rotting planks, almost black in colour. The wallpaper had mostly fallen off revealing the bricks beneath, and in the places where it still stood mould was spreading. He looked at the mould for a few moments, those black dots congregating, then his eyes were pulled back onto her.

Contrary to those on the outside, a flame was burning inside her eyes, but it was not one kindled by life, but one kindled by the certainty of a soon end.

"I brought you some fresh water and something to eat. I know it's not much, but… I hope you'll feel better soon." – his expression seemed indecisive, somewhere in between a forced smile and deepfelt pity.

"Thank you." – she said with a smile, bleak in appearance, for she had not the strength for more – "I hope I don't. All I hope for is a soon end. I'm tired of this life. So awfully tired."

K. shook his head: "I know you're saying it only because you're in pain. But you will get better soon, back to the old you. You are like a sister to me. I'll take care of you." – he spoke, but there was treachery rooted in his intention, infesting every attempt for sincerity.

"No… I don't just mean this disease which is rotting away my body. It's this whole life that I'm tired of. The disease which is rotting human hearts is the one thing I cannot stand anymore."

"Yes, the world is a god-awful place, but don't let their diseased hearts become your poison."

She gave out a broken laugh which ended in a cough, and then she said: "The poison is in the very air you breathe. From the moment you are born, it infests your heart, slowly rotting it away. And if by chance you're able to withstand that poison, their envy and despair will be the cause of your ruin. Nothing can stand against the flame of jealousy which is burning inside of them."

"Nor the real flames they ignite." – he said with sorrow in his voice

"I'm sorry. I didn't mean to remind you of her death."

"Don't worry. I cannot escape my grief and I don't want to. It's the one thing that keeps me pushing forward."

"Oh, what a sweet ego you got. To use one's downfall for your own benefit. Not so unlike to that which they are doing."

"What my ego does in simple survival – finding meaning in the meaningless. What they do is sheer madness fuelled by angst."

"Tell me, how do they become what they are?"

"They couldn't find meaning, faced with the meaningless miasma. Thus, an abysmal angst took hold of their egos and turned them into beasts."

"And why do they do what they do?" – she asked, but he remained silent, looking at his feet – "It is simple survival – finding meaning in the meaningless. Am I not right? But it is more than that. If your heart is pure, you will not fall to the id, but if it is diseased, there is no stopping for the id to take hold of your ego. But how does a heart become inflicted by disease?" – she shook her head – "I'm sorry. There is no need for you to listen to my rambling. It is just that now, when my body has betrayed me, the only thing I can do is contemplate."

"I do not mind at all." – he looked at her with a smile – "I really want to hear your thoughts. After all, that's all that will soon be left of you."

"How true. So, what is the cause of that disease which takes hold of our hearts? It's desire… From birth on we want, and the more we get, the more we want. As babies we only desire the touch of our mother, thus we cry out and do not stop until we feel her worm touch. And although motivated by nothing but the best of intentions, her embrace fuels the flame of the ego. And in the moment of fulfilment, a desire loses its sweetness – it melts away like a snowflake at the touch of a hand. But the ego is made of desire, so when one vanishes, another ignites. A never-ending journey, where every desire, satisfied or still burning, is a building block of the self. Everything we obtained and everything which is still to be obtained makes us who we are. But our hearts need boundaries, or else they will be consumed by the flames of desire. The desire for the mother's touch turns into the desire for the touch of a lover; one lover turns into two, and two into ten. The desire to still our hunger turns into the desire to enjoy the taste which either turns into gluttony or endless tailoring of the taste. The desire for shelter turns into the desire for comfort, which escalates endlessly. And as you can see, all desires lead into decadence. We want more, we want better. The ego cannot be satiated. And similar to that old saying 'If you have no worries in life, put a small stone in your shoe, so it may bother you.', they, when all desires are satisfied, embark on creating new problems, but without restrain, it only spirals out of control creating pure madness in the process. And now, that they have met with the ultimate restrain, they desire to overcome it, but fail miserably. However, as beings who have never known limits, they do not know how to deal with that restrain, making it possible for the id to take hold of the last fragments of their egos, exposing their true nature – their rotten hearts."

And long after leaving, her words still echoed in K.'s head. How much alike was he to them? How much was his heart diseased? Are his actions truly out of pure necessity or is he just deluding himself?

He knew he was not a righteous man, not without sin, but not a beast either. And although he could give into his ego, he still held onto his humanity.

Not all desires corrupt, he was sure of that. How could it be wrong to seek out pleasure, in one form or another, if no one was harmed in the process? And even the deeds of more moral ambiguity – if no harm was done, or if they were even done for the sake of good – how heavy could they weigh on someone's heart?

If it wasn't for his work, he would not be alive. The boy with his two siblings would probably not be alive either. That friend of his sister would live out her last days in misery, same as that old woman would have done, if it wasn't for his help.

And so, he made himself believe that he was good, that he was not like everyone else.

That old woman's house was his next destination. Now that she had died, there was only one thing left for him to do.

The sun had already started to fall, as he approached her house. And he had to be fast if he was to make it back home before the sirens wake. Carefully, to not get heard by anyone, he ascended the wooden stairs. Every step he took gave out a shrieking noise. His heart was beating faster. There was no telling what might happen to him if he gets caught.

He slowly opened the door, barely enough so he could squeeze inside. For a moment he just stood in the darkened hallway. He knew there was no one inside and yet he felt observed. In this apartment as well, the air was stale, but more acidic in smell. He thought it to be cold and wet inside as if standing in autumn rain. His eyes moved from left to right. Everything seemed the same as it was the last time he came.

Yesterday as he came to visit, he found the collectors taking her dead body away, so he simply walked away. He had felt anxious that someone might not pre-empt him, but now a feeling of ease overcame him, for no one else had done K.'s deed.

In the bedroom, to his left, there was nothing but a bed. The sheets on it carrying the marks which the old woman left in her moments of death.

The bathroom, to his right, had nothing of value either, so he moved to the living room which opened in front of him.

Thick curtains were drawn on the windows. There was no light besides a few lambent rays that pierced through the darkened room while particles of dust were dancing gracefully inside of them.

In the middle of the room a table was placed and around it a sofa and an armchair were aligned. On one side there was a wall with photos and on the other a massive wooden cabinet. On it more photos, a few plates, some crystal glasses, and a candle holder.

In one of the drawers, K. found a necklace and a couple of wedding rings. In another a few coins.

On a small bookshelf, he found three books: The Plague by Albert Camus, The Master and Margarita by Mikhail Bulgakov, and Crime and Punishment by Fyodor Dostoyevsky.

Everything but the photos K. put in a bag and left hastily.

Overcome by feelings of transience K. walked the streets clinging to his bag.

The old woman always seemed overcome by joy when K. visited. Her greatest sorrow was the early death of her husband and her greatest fear to be faced with death all on her own. What dread must she have felt in those last moments all alone in that cold and dark room.

Although he would not admit it, K. was terrified of death. As much as he hated life, he did not want to die. At least not in solitude abandoned by everyone. He hated the sirens not because of the sound itself, but because they were a reminder of his mortality and solitude. During the day he was surrounded by people, even though strangers, but at night he was alone left to his fear.

And with every step he took, the dread in him rose for soon the sirens would wake and leave him in the dark to endure his pain.

So many times, had he cried and screamed in silence, throughout the night, whilst shivering in fear, as he hoped for the morning to come.

So many times, had he thought of taking his own life, to at least die on his own terms, but he couldn't bring himself to do so. His resolve was, every time, only skin deep. And after each failed attempt there was only more scars on his wrists, just to mock his cowardness.

As K. approached his apartment, the setting sun was barely visible behind the buildings. Brimming with life this morning, the street was now desolated; all but for one boy – barely eighteen – who stood in front of the entrance to K.'s apartment.

"Thomas!" – K. exclaimed as he ran towards the boy – "What are you doing here?"

The boy's anxious expression turned into a wide smile at the sound of that familiar voice: "For two days I haven't heard anything from you, so I got worried. I'm sorry. I guess it was silly of me to worry."

"On the contrary. I'm happy to see you. Please come in."

"It's almost curfew time and I have to go back to my siblings."

The happiness faded from K.'s face as he was overcome by dread anew: I beg you. Only for tonight. Please stay with me. I can't bear to be alone another night."

Seeing the pain in K.'s eyes Thomas agreed reluctantly knowing that his siblings would be safe even without him for one night.

Deep into the night, K. stood at the window observing the world covered in dark. Bleak light scattered throughout a few windows and the pale moon seemed like the only light in existence. In it, flakes of ash danced their macabre dance.

"You seem to be better now." – said Thomas still lying in the bed

"I'm sorry. You really shouldn't have seen me like that." – K. looked at Thomas with a pained smile; his body exposed as created by God.

"Don't misunderstand me, but I'm glad I did. If I know about your struggle, I can try and help you." – Thomas moved his hand over the bed indicating for K. to sit down.

K. moved away from the window and sat down at the edge of the bed and then spoke: "It's just that sometimes I get overwhelmed by some kind of feelings. I can't really put a name on them, but it feels heavy on my chest. It gets hard to breathe and it starts to pain."

Thomas embraced him from behind, putting his head onto K.'s shoulder: "I will always be here if you need me. There is no need to keep it all for yourself."

A faint smile appeared on K.'s face as he turned towards Thomas: "Maybe you could move in here with your siblings. I mean, there is enough space, and it is more secure and you wouldn't need to work anymore, at least you could do something different."

With a gentle voice, Thomas called K. by his name and said: "I would like to move here… with you."

Overcome by joy K. embraced Thomas.

"Do you think that my work is bad?" – asked Thomas

"I don't think I'm the right person to talk about good and bad work. You do what you can to provide for your siblings. So, it certainly serves some good. And on a personal note, if it wasn't for that work we surely wouldn't have met. But you must be careful. Hold onto your humanity. Don't let those deeds corrupt your soul."

Thomas shook his head: "Don't worry. It's just work. I don't do it because I like to do it, but because it's the only way for my siblings to survive. If I can be honest with you, I've cried myself to sleep many times, disgusted by what I've done. But when I think of those two monkeys, I have no other choice but to continue. I dread the thought of losing them."

"I understand your feelings and that's why I'm saying it. No matter how noble your intentions might be, a sin will taint your soul. And the more your soul gets tainted, the more of your humanity you lose. And fear is just fuel for that process."

"Do you think that we still have some humanity left in us?"

"For certain. But it becomes rather difficult to tell how much humanity is left in you when everyone around you is a sinner. You could be the worst of them, but think yourself a saint."

Thomas looked into K.'s eyes, his own twinkling with joy, and said: "Even if you were to lose all your humanity, I would still be there for you. As long as I have my siblings and you, I don't need anything else in my life."

*

As the burning pain throbs in my stomach, the curtains fall for me onto the stage of this wretched world.

I sit in the dark, abandoned by the one I love, as he fled in terror at the realization of his action.

And all that's left for me to do is to greet death as have these two creatures, lying next to me, in the night past.

Oh, I'm so frightened!

But you, don't be. Don't despair. Don't let our deaths be in vain. Live on and remember us, and we will live on in your memory.

No…

Remember them, but not me. I am the one who told you to stay. If it wasn't for me, you wouldn't be in that pain right now.

And don't feel guilt for my demise, for I brought it upon myself. If I had stayed and waited, after my wake, when I did not find you in my bed, I still would be a part of this play. Your action was but a reflex done in fright and grief. No wrong has been done on your part, but all of it is on me.

Sweet death, tell me; have I lost my humanity? Have I turned into a beast like all the others have? How much wrong have I done blinded by my self-righteous ego?

Oh, sweet death come and take me now. Take away my pain and suffering. Save what's left of my soul, if anything at all. Take me now, for I do not wish to witness his saddened face, once he returns.

What a fitting end this is for a wretched creature like me.

Agapenoria

Once upon a time, in some city of some country, I walked alone one winter morning. As the cold bit my cheeks, dirty snow hid in the fog, and the clamour of people and the noise of vehicles disrupted the idyll of weary hearts. And as I wandered lost in unfamiliar streets, I saw an old man standing alone. Clad in a black coat and black boots, he was like a statue estranged from the world. Upon his shoulders and outstretched hands, as if in prayer, doves descended. Enchanted by this sight, I was unable not to conceive the paths of destiny that led him to that moment.

Like any other, his childhood was filled with ignorance. Blinded by his naivety, he walked in Elysian gardens that were nestled within the embrace of hell. As an only child, he enjoyed the unparalleled love of his mother, and also his father, in those rare moments when he was home. They didn't have much, and what little they had, war disputed day by day. And upon its end, the mother's sacrifice was dearly paid. Her death, the first taste of pain, and the loss of paradise for the innocent boy.

The father, once seemingly gentle and caring, grew harsher and more distant with each passing day. He would come home regularly drunk - cursing, singing, then cursing again. In moments of sobriety, he would teach his son the piano, only to beat him when alcohol clouded his mind. Paradise was no longer even a memory for the boy; robbed of happiness, he endured an existence he did not desire.

And so the years passed, and the boy grew up, and with youth came the winds of change. Not just physical; it was also a period marked by the initial success of a young pianist, but also a period of awakening to first love.

She was a beautiful girl - a fragile angel in his eyes. He would spend his days thinking of her, and in nights he would dream of her. She was his muse, the source of his happiness, and his friend. Yes, his friend – nothing more than a friend. Her heart belonged to another, and as a good friend, he supported her love. And all his pain, all the suffering of his heart, he poured into music.

With time, he became a brilliant virtuoso, and his name was celebrated in the highest circles of society. At the peak of his career, he was given the opportunity to perform a solo concert in the most prestigious concert hall in the country.

That evening, all the seats were filled, except one. Only the love of his life, his pain, was absent.

But his heart was not discouraged. Every composition, every played note, was dedicated to her – an anthem to the girl who belonged to another.

At that moment, only the gods knew that he would never play again after that evening. The night of his success – his fame – was actually the night of his downfall. It was the night his muse lost her life.

The only reason he did not escort her into death was...

And the years passed. His life became mere existence. Agony. Gloomy greyness without a glimmer of light. And as old age caught up with him, shackled in misery, he found solace in doves. In those fleeting moments, he felt peace; a brief breath of paradise before returning to hell.

Requiem

Sacrifices and prayers of praise, Lord,
we offer to You.
Receive them in behalf of those souls
we commemorate today.
And let them, Lord,
pass from death to life,
which was promised to Abraham
and his descendants.

The gloomy sun penetrated through the dirtened glass of the window, and falling onto the faded wooden floor it crawled over the same, reaching, with its elongated bony fingers, to the body which laid on the bed.

That body, that miserable creature, whose name is not worth the mention, completely awake – without a moment of sleep in the night past, as in countless nights before – observed a worm, standing on the glass, as it looked at the world around it as if seeing it for the first time.

And in that moment, he felt envy towards the worm and he spoke: "What do you see in this world, which you haven't seen before, and it being worth your admiration?"

After some time, he sighed painfully, as if truly expecting an answer; as if insulted for not getting the same. But what worth does an answer carry, if the questioner is unable to accept it; if he is unable to understand its truth? As if a creature, who spent its life in the vastness of the colourless wastelands, was able to understand the awe that a worm feels towards a colourful flower?

Ignoring all the sublimity of existence, all the splendour of infinite human potential, he gave in to the lowest of passions, which only had to touch him with its breath. And after the deed was done – as in countless mornings before – after the passion has left his embrace again, he looked at the dirtened hand, his mind obliterated, and only one question lurking in that dark; Why?

And as countless times before, fate wanted the same morning to repeat itself again.

In one moment, as his thoughts returned anew, he rose from his grave of reclusion with the intention to wash off the traces from his hand, and those from his mind; all till the next morning when the same was to repeat itself, as countless mornings before.

And as countless times before, this morning as well, he forced himself to leave that cage which he built up himself in the middle of the wasteland (to protect himself from the heartless beasts that lurked outside) in search of that which he did not believe to exist.

In his futile search, he witnessed various atrocities that existed in the vastness of that desolation, knowing that atrocities even more horrifying remained hidden from his numb gaze.

The beasts, who treaded the wasteland, were grey, tall and thin creatures without faces, and when passing a glass structure, in the corner of his eye, he would see that he was one of them.

Those creatures would bind their females with chains, and completely naked, the females would crawl over the ground on all fours.

They would eat one another, and vomiting what they have eaten, others would eat that.

Under the watchful eye of Apollo, unhidden from others, they would merge into one, and after separating anew they would depart in search of others and in search of fleeting union.

And in the rare cases, when the desire for a lasting bond awakens inside of them, through the use of a needle and rusty wire, they bind their bodies to each other, only to tear the bonds (tearing the flesh of the other) when their desire passes.

This poor creature was offered a bond once as well, but in fear of the pain he rejected the offer.

Some of the creatures would even sit under the trees, and feasting on its fruits they would become oblivious to the desolation around them.

And there were even those that hid colour inside of their chests, as did this poor creature.

Truly disgusting beasts.

Yet, this morning wasn't as countless mornings before. Taken over by drowsiness, he sank into a dream far from all the beasts – devoted only to himself and to Apollo, who cruelly reigned from above.

Enjoying the sweet fruits of dream, he heard a voice calling for him. Not wanting to lose those fruits, he turned a deaf ear to the calls, but was torn from that paradise by two hands, finding himself eye-to-eye with beauty.

"Who are you?" – he asked

"By my father, I was bestowed with the name Calliope, and with pride I wear it. But who are you?" – she asked

"I do not know." – he answered, turning his gaze away from her. The place, on which he fell asleep, was desolation no more, but a fertile meadow. He was deeply sank into green grass, as the merciful Apollo illuminated him with mild light.

"Know!" – she commanded, and asked again – "Who are you?"

"I don't know."

"Who are you?"

"I am nobody." – he answered in defeat

Unsatisfied with his answer, she lowered her lips onto his, and he welcomed them, inviting her whole into a union with him.

Fragile eternity hid itself in every moment of their union, begetting countless worlds and destroying countless.

And later, as the blissful sun covered them with its rays, Calliope, with her long thin fingers, reached towards him, who was lying among colourful flowers. He was observing a butterfly, coming out of its cocoon, spreading its colourful wings in spite to the world.

"Who are you?" – she asked again

And he, with a triumphant smile, which defied the world answered: "I am stardust moulded into an effigy and a soul embedded into that raging abyss. Potential unleashed, burning bright like a newborn star. I am a devoted slave to the Almighty Lord. Freed of shackles I bow to none – no creation, no heart's desire. I am the son of Algea and the brother of Nihilis. I am a lover to the Muses. I am the Artist. I am the sacrifice with the knife at the throat, waiting to be slaughtered for the collective, I am the one slaughtering it for the blooming ego. I am the wonderer. A student of the world, and a teacher to the world. I am a dreamer, getting drunk with my nightly adventures. I am a candle in the wind and a rock in the blustering waves. I am earth touching the earth and a thousand worlds burning in an instant. Born in the sign of Mars I am a seedling in the search of the self."

www.ingramcontent.com/pod-product-compliance
Lightning Source LLC
Chambersburg PA
CBHW051443140726
47987CB00006B/2522